TINY PIE

by **Mark Bailey** and **Michael Oatman**

illustrated by Edward Hemingway

Recipe by
Alice Waters

WITHDRAWN

RP KIDS
PHILADELPHIA · LONDON

Books published by Running Press are available at special discounts for bulk purchases in the United States by
corporations, institutions, and other organizations. For more information, please contact the Special Markets
Department at the Perseus Books Group, 2300 Chestnut Street, Suite 200, Philadelphia, PA 19103, or call
(800) 810-4145, ext. 5000, or e-mail special.markets@perseusbooks.com.

ISBN 978-0-7624-4482-3

Library of Congress Control Number: 2012946110

9 8 7 6 5 4 3 2 1
Digit on the right indicates the number of this printing

Designed by Frances J. Soo Ping Chow
Edited by Marlo Scrimizzi
Typography: Champagne & Limousines, Denne Milk Tea,
Lobster Two, and Mostly Mono

Published by Running Press Kids
An Imprint of Running Press Book Publishers
A Member of the Perseus Books Group
2300 Chestnut Street
Philadelphia, PA 19103-4371

Visit us on the web!
www.runningpress.com/kids

For Georgia, Bridget, and Zachary,
my own slice of heaven.
—MB

For Matthew and Katherine, Gordon, and Ann,
now please go to sleep as fast as you can.
—MO

To Melinda and Les Tyler,
who are the BEST.
—EH

The entire **TINY PIE** team thanks Alice Waters for so generously
donating her delicious Tiny Apple Pie recipe to this book!

ONCE UPON A NIGHTTIME,
there was a party on Elephant Lane.

It was not a birthday party, a holiday party, or a tea party.
It was a grown-up party—you know—for big people.

But for little people, there was little fun.
And for little Ellie, there was none. She had been told
to stay out of the way—or else go to bed.

She chose *not* to go to bed.

Then Ellie got hungry. She knew this because her tummy told her so. It said, *rumble, rumble, rumble.*

Ellie asked her mother, "Mama? *Oopa, doopa, doo?*"
"Shush, Ellie," said her mother. "Please stay out of the way.
This is a grown-up party."

She asked her father, "*Dada? Stoopa, loopa, loo?*"

"Ellie, I think it's time for bed," said her father.
"You are too little to be up so late."

But, *rumble, rumble, rumble!* said Ellie's stomach again.

She was still hungry.

Ellie walked into the kitchen.

If only she was tall enough to reach the counter.
Then she could reach the cookie jar.

If only she was strong enough to open the freezer.
Then she could grab an ice cream bar.

But it seemed as though everything was for big people. . . .

Or was it?

"HELLO OUT THERE IN TV LAND!
Welcome to *Hole in the Kitchen Wall*.
A cooking show for everyone, especially the small.

In this episode, we are going to bake,
in just under an hour,
A tasty treat, savory and sweet,
that starts with unbleached flour.

"Now I can see you wondering, *Is this something I can do?*
But if you're big enough to eat dessert, then you can make it too.

APPLAUSE

"So if anyone big ever comes up
to you and asks . . .

'What good are your tiny eyes?
What can you see?'

"Just tell them you see . . .

'Paws with itsy-bitsy claws,
As busy as can be.'

"And if they ask . . .

'What good are your tiny ears?
What can you hear?'

"Tell them you hear . . .

'Apples on a chopping block—
But please be careful, dear.'

"And if they ask . . .
'What good is your tiny nose?
What can you sniff?'

"Tell them you smell . . .

'Melted butter and cinnamon,
Why don't you take a whiff?'

"And if they ask . . .

'What good are your tiny hands?
What can you touch?'

"You say . . .

'It's round and warm and very small,
Just don't take too much.'

"And when they ask . . .

'What good is your tiny mouth?
What can you taste?'

"Shout out . . .
'IT'S TINY PIE! IT'S TINY PIE!
It sure won't go to waste.'

"Now come and join our party at *Hole in the Kitchen Wall*.
Where a pie was made in under an hour,
by bakers not so tall.

"Your friends are here, in best of cheer, and they are glad to say,
Parties are for everyone because we all know how to play.

"And if anyone ever asks . . .

'What good is your tiny heart?
What can you wish?'

"Just tell them . . .

"Whether you are big, small, short, or tall,
you will always find your perfect dish."

And they baked happily ever after....

Would you like to bake a Tiny Pie because it's something you can do? Follow Alice Waters' recipe, written especially for you.

Be sure to ask a grown-up for help!

TINY APPLE PIES

by Alice Waters

This recipe makes 6 tiny apple pies. It involves 2 separate steps: making the dough and making the pie.

Step 1:

Crunch Dough

UTENSILS

Large mixing bowl

Stirring spoon

Kitchen knife

Pastry cutter

Small bowl

Plastic wrap

INGREDIENTS

2 cups of unbleached all-purpose flour

5 tablespoons of sugar

$1/4$ teaspoon of salt

12 tablespoons or $1^1/2$ sticks of cold, unsalted butter

7 tablespoons of ice water

1. Put the flour, sugar, and salt into a large mixing bowl and stir them together with a spoon. Slice the butter into small squares. Add half of the squares to the flour bowl. Then using your fingers, lightly toss the butter in the flour.

2. Using a pastry cutter (a helpful tool to cut butter), cut the butter into the flour until it looks like oatmeal. Then add the rest of the butter squares to the bowl and lightly toss them in the flour (just like before). Using the pastry cutter again, cut the butter into the flour until the larger pieces are about the size of lima beans.

3. Fill a small bowl with ice water. Drizzle 7 tablespoons of ice water into the bowl, one tablespoon at a time, and lightly toss the dough between your fingers. Keep tossing the dough until it starts to stick together, but still has some dry patches in it. Then gather the dough together and gently press it into the shape of a brick.

4. Cut the dough into 6 even pieces, about 3 ounces each. Wrap each piece of dough in plastic wrap, and press each package with your hand into a flat disc. Put the dough in the refrigerator for at least 30 minutes.

UTENSILS

2 baking sheets
Parchment paper
Rolling pin
Paring knife or peeler
Kitchen knife
Small bowl
Basting brush (optional)

INGREDIENTS

Unbleached all-purpose flour
   for sprinkling
3 small to medium apples
   (about 1 pound total).
   We recommend Sierra
   Beauty or Pippin apples.
2 tablespoons of melted
   unsalted butter
1 teaspoon of sugar
$\frac{1}{4}$ teaspoon of ground
   cinnamon

Step 2:
Apple Pie

1. Heat the oven to 400°F.

2. Line 2 baking sheets with parchment paper. Sprinkle your work surface with flour. After the dough has been in the refrigerator for at least 30 minutes, remove it. You will be rolling out one disc of dough at a time.

3. Using a rolling pin, roll the disc of dough into a slightly larger circle, about 7 inches across and $\frac{1}{8}$ inch thick. Brush off any extra flour and carefully transfer the circle to one of the baking sheets. Repeat the process with the other discs, placing them on the baking sheets so they do not touch one another. Then put the baking sheets of dough in the refrigerator while you peel and cut the apples.

4. Peel the apples and chop them into quarters (4 pieces). Remove the cores and cut the apples into slices about $\frac{1}{4}$ inch thick. Mix the sugar and cinnamon together in a small bowl. Then take the baking sheets of dough out of the refrigerator.

5. Arrange the apples in a ring in the center of each circle of dough; you want the apple slices to overlap a little as you stack them on top of each other. Leave a 1 $\frac{1}{2}$-inch-wide border around the apples (for the crust). Fold the edge of the dough over the apples of each tiny pie, making pleats here and there. Then brush the apples and the rims of the pies with the melted butter, and evenly sprinkle the cinnamon-sugar over the apples and dough.

6. Bake the pies in the lower third of the oven for about 35 minutes, until the apples are tender and the crust is golden brown. When the pies are done, let them cool slightly before eating. Enjoy!